NUTBURY

NEW PORK

WEST CHEDDAR

Officer KATZ and HOUNDINI
A Tale of Two Tails

by MARIA GIANFERRARI ✴ illustrated by DANNY CHATZIKONSTANTINOU

ALADDIN

New York London Toronto Sydney New Delhi

ALADDIN

An imprint of Simon & Schuster Children's Publishing Division • 1230 Avenue of the Americas, New York, NY 10020 • First Aladdin hardcover edition October 2016 • Text copyright © 2016 by Maria Gianferrari • Illustrations copyright © 2016 by Danny Chatzikonstantinou • All rights reserved, including the right of reproduction in whole or in part in any form. • ALADDIN is a trademark of Simon & Schuster, Inc., and related logo is a registered trademark of Simon & Schuster, Inc. • For information about special discounts for bulk purchases, please contact Simon & Schuster Special Sales at 1-866-506-1949 or business@simonandschuster.com.

The Simon & Schuster Speakers Bureau can bring authors to your live event. For more information or to book an event contact the Simon & Schuster Speakers Bureau at 1-866-248-3049 or visit our website at www.simonspeakers.com. • Book designed by Laura Lyn DiSiena • The illustrations for this book were rendered digitally. • The text of this book was set in Brandon Grotesque. • Manufactured in China 0716 SCP • 10 9 8 7 6 5 4 3 2 1 This book has been cataloged with the Library of Congress.

ISBN 978-1-4814-2265-9 (hc)
ISBN 978-1-4814-2266-6 (eBook)

In memory of Gretchen Holt Allen, and her Rebecca
—M. G.

To the amazing Kyra and Phoebe
—D. C.

Officer Katz was an inventor extraordinaire.
His Katz-traptions were the best in Kitty City.

But even with the help of Deputy Catbird,
Officer Katz could not catch the
Great Houndini. . . .

Houndini's traveling show, The Great Escape, returned each year to Kitty City. Every time, Houndini marked Davy Crock-cat's portrait before eluding capture. None of Officer Katz's feline forebears had ever captured Houndini.

Officer Katz was retiring. It was his last chance to collar the Great Houndini and teach that old dog some new tricks.

Houndini hurtled into town,
tipping his top hat,
his cape billowing in the breeze.

Houndini and Squirrel set up the tent in Kitty City Square.

Kitty City's citizens filled the seats.

Paw-parazzi lined the aisles.

Houndini hightailed it out of handcuffs.
The crowd oohed.

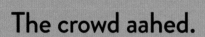

Houndini skedaddled
out of the stocks.

The crowd aahed.

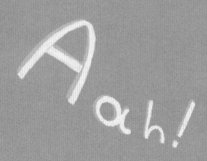

Houndini wrestled out of ropes

and burst free from boxes.

The crowd oohed and aahed,
and oohed some more.

Ooh!

Aah!

Ooh!

Houndini clipped his cape and tipped his top hat.

But it was the same show, city after city, year after year.

"WAIT!" shouted Officer Katz as the curtain closed.

He twirled his Katz-rope like a lasso.

"I'll give you three chances to escape me. *When* I win, you'll have to flee Kitty City, call off the dogs, and never return again."

Houndini's hair began to prickle.

His top hat tipped.

His tail wagged.

"You're on!" said Houndini. "But when *I* win, I'll be
top dog, you'll grow a mustache, and Kitty City will become . . ."

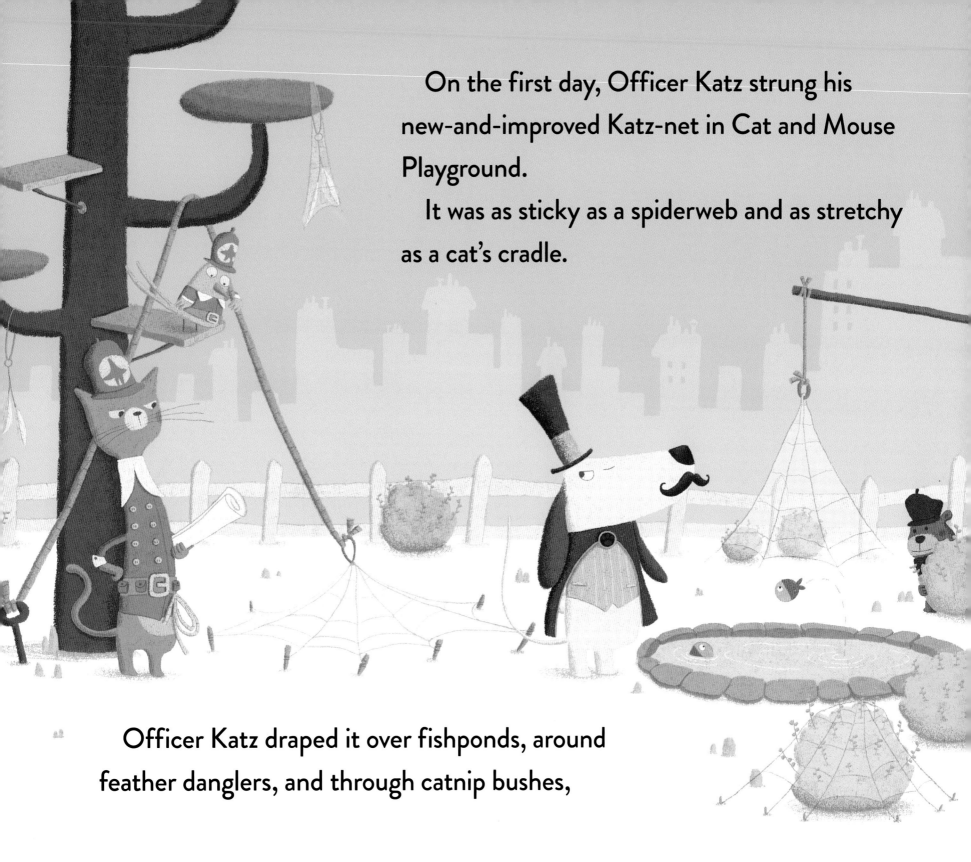

On the first day, Officer Katz strung his new-and-improved Katz-net in Cat and Mouse Playground.

It was as sticky as a spiderweb and as stretchy as a cat's cradle.

Officer Katz draped it over fishponds, around feather danglers, and through catnip bushes,

and then coiled it around Houndini.

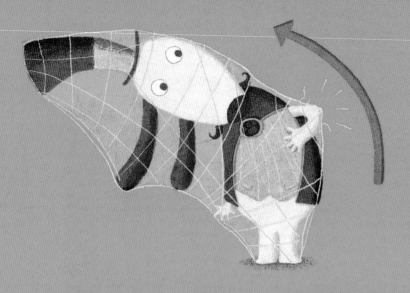

Houndini rolled to the left;

Houndini unrolled to the right.

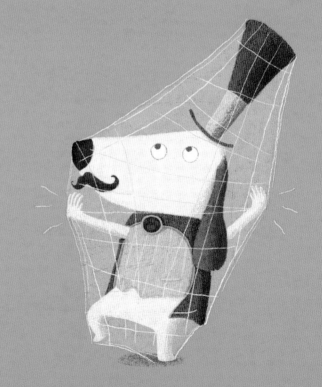

Houndini twisted and turned, but he was wrapped and trapped.

TABBY TIMES

NOT THE KATZ MEOW

Officer Katz straightened his cap and posed for the paw-parazzi.

Until, with a bow and a wow and a tip of his top hat, Houndini disappeared.

Poof!

Like magic.

On day two, Officer Katz showed off his
Katz-box invention in Tidy Kitty Litter Park.
The Katz-box was a maze within a cube.

"My Katz-box will put Houndini in the doghouse!"
said Officer Katz to the paw-parazzi.

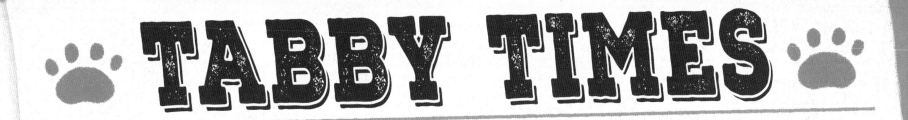

TABBY TIMES

WHO LET THE DOG OUT?–WOOF, WOOF!

Officer Katz straightened his cap and posed for the paw-parazzi.

Until, with a bow and a wow and a tip of his top hat, Houndini disappeared.

Poof!

Like magic.

On day three, Officer Katz constructed the Katz-apult in the gardens of Scratch Pole Palace.
It was his prized invention.
Houndini would soar through the sky.

There was no way even he could make a midair escape.
"The cat's definitely in the bag this time!" said Officer Katz to the paw-parazzi.

Houndini stepped into the sack.

Officer Katz secured the cinch.

He pulled the rope taut.

The sack slid lower.

And lower.

1...2...3...

BLAST OFF!

Whoops!

Officer Katz did not pose;

Houndini did not tip his top hat.

The crowd roared and clapped for more.

The paw-parazzi snapped picture after picture.

READ ALL ABOUT IT!

TABBY TIMES

KATZ AND HOUNDINI
ARE IN THE BAG!

"My Katz-apult is kaput," said Officer Katz.

"Hot diggity dog, you caught me!" barked Houndini.

"I did, didn't I?" said Officer Katz.

"And the crowd loves it," said Houndini. "Let's stop
fighting like cats and dogs and take our show on the road."
Officer Katz and Houndini shook paws.

"I have one more trick up my sleeve," said Houndini. "Presto chango!"

And they both disappeared.

Poof!

Like magic.

Officer Katz and Houndini took their show on the road,
with a little help from Squirrel and Deputy Catbird.
Next stop, Dogtown.

THE GREAT ESCAPE II

DOGTOWN

MANE